THE HORSELOVER'S HANDBOOK:

AN INTRODUCTION TO OWNING, CARING FOR, AND RIDING HORSES

About the Author

Leda Blumberg trains horses, teaches riding, runs a small stable, and competes in horse shows. When not riding or caring for horses, she is usually writing about them. She has written numerous magazine articles about horsemanship and horse care. She is author of *Pets,* a reference book for young people, and is coauthor of *The Simon and Schuster Book of Facts and Fallacies.*

About the Photographer

Murray Tinkelman, artist and photographer, has received over 150 major professional awards. His work is represented in the permanent collections of the Brooklyn Museum and the Smithsonian Institution. Horses are his favorite subject, and he has written and illustrated three books about rodeo. Mr. Tinkelman, who lectures widely, is a professor of illustration at Syracuse University in Syracuse, New York.

THE HORSELOVER'S HANDBOOK:

AN INTRODUCTION TO OWNING, CARING FOR, AND RIDING HORSES

LEDA BLUMBERG

PHOTOGRAPHS BY
MURRAY TINKELMAN

THE HORSELOVER'S HANDBOOK is an original publication of Avon Books. This work has never before appeared in book form.

6th grade reading level has been determined by using the Fry Readability Scale.

AVON BOOKS
A division of
The Hearst Corporation
1790 Broadway
New York, New York 10019

Published by arrangement with the author
Library of Congress Catalog Card Number: 84-45322
ISBN: 0-380-89326-6

First Camelot Printing, November 1984

Printed in the U.S.A.

OPB 10 9 8 7 6 5 4 3 2

For my original stablemates,
Larry, Rena, and Alice

L. B.

For Ronni and Susan

M. T.

Contents

INTRODUCTION

A Horse of Your Own

For as long as I can remember, I have always dreamed of owning my own horse. When I was a young child, I collected model horses and "played horse" by jumping over my parents' lawn furniture. Every horse I saw made me "ooh" and "ah." (I still do.) And nothing sounded more wonderful than having a horse of my own.

When I was fourteen, my dream came true. A beautiful white horse called Mommy came into my life. She was sweet, lovable, and a joy to ride. Along with the fun and excitement of having my own horse came work and responsibility. Mommy needed my care and attention every day. She had to be fed, groomed, and exercised. I had barn work to do and heavy water buckets to carry. But it was wonderful—the best thing that ever happened to me.

My love of horses has never faded. Today I run a small stable, teach horseback riding, train horses, and compete in horse shows. When not riding or caring for horses, I am usually writing about them. As I write, I can gaze out my window and look at my

The author and her horse, Damascus.

horse, Damascus. His sleek, dark-red coat shimmers in the sun as he contentedly munches on grass. When I ride him, I am on top of the world.

Murray, who took the photographs for this book, has always loved horses, too. As a teenager, he owned a lovely golden-colored horse named Champagne. Together, Murray and Champagne roamed the wooded trails every day after school. They were close friends.

Although Murray no longer owns a horse, he spends a lot of time photographing and drawing them. Big or little, shaggy or sleek, he loves them all. Every horse is a beautiful creature worthy of an artist's attention.

Many people dream of owning their own horses. Owning one is a real joy, but it is also a lot of work.

You must be willing to devote part of every day to your horse. Your large friend will depend on you for food, shelter, grooming, and exercise. Owning a horse takes time, money, work, and daily devotion.

Some days you won't feel like going out into the pouring rain or the bitter cold to care for your horse. Sitting in a nice warm house with your favorite music playing may be cozier. But your horse relies on you. You must be willing to care for him whatever the weather and whatever your mood.

Taking care of a horse can be a great pleasure. Much of the work is fun, and you and your horse can become close friends and good companions. It feels good to come into the barn on a snowy winter morning—to have a velvety muzzle to pat and to talk to a four-footed friend who will listen to everything you have to say.

CHAPTER ONE

Buying a Horse

Before buying a horse, learn as much as you can about riding and horse care. You can take riding

An experienced horse person should help beginners choose their first horse or pony.

lessons at a local stable. And you can learn about horse care at a 4-H Club, Pony Club, riding camp, or stable—and by reading this book. Then ask yourself these questions.

- Why do I want a horse?
- Where will I keep my horse?
- How much time can I devote to a horse?
- What type of riding would I like to do? Do I want a horse for Western riding, English riding, trail rides, horse shows, jumping, or just plain backyard fun?

A horse will take up a lot of your time, so it is important that you buy the right one. Seek the advice of a horse expert who can help you choose an animal that will be well suited to your riding ability.

When you look at a horse you may buy, observe its behavior around the stable. (Is he gentle and friendly? Is he stubborn or lazy?) Then, before you climb aboard, watch someone else ride him. Finally, try him yourself. Can you control the horse? Does he respond to you?

Ask about his background. Has the horse been raced, shown, ridden English or Western? You will want to buy a horse that is trained for the type of riding you prefer.

When you find a horse you like, ride him several times before making your final decision. The more time you spend with your prospective mount, the better. If you intend to use the horse for trail riding, ride him on some trails. If you want a jumper, watch someone jump the horse, then jump him yourself.

In the excitement of choosing your own horse, it is easy to fall in love with anything that has four legs and a tail. However, it is very important that you take time to choose carefully. The animal's age, size, breed, sex, temperament, and training must all be considered.

What to Look For When You Buy a Horse

Age: How Old a Horse Do You Want?

Usually older, well-trained horses make the best first horses. Young *foals* (baby horses) are adorable, but they are hard to train. Only a very experienced rider should buy a young horse that needs training.

Healthy, well-cared-for horses usually live for twenty to thirty years. The oldest horse recorded, Old Billy, lived for sixty-two years!

Size: How Big Should Your Horse Be?

A horse's height is measured in *hands,* not feet. One hand equals four inches, the average width of a man's hand. Horses are measured for height at their *withers,* the bony area where the neck joins the back.

If you are less than fourteen years old, you may want a pony. Older teenagers and adults will probably want a larger horse. Ponies aren't young horses. They are types or breeds of horses that are small in

Little Lady, a small pony, is a good size for Debbie (left) and Christie to learn on, but soon they will be too big to ride her.

size when they are fully grown. Ponies are less than 14½ hands (58 inches) high.

Whatever size animal you choose, it should be small enough to mount by yourself and large enough so that your legs don't hang beneath its belly.

What Breed Should You Pick?

People have been developing different types or breeds of horses for at least 3,000 years. Selected horses are bred together to produce breeds for pleasure, work, beauty, speed, and athletic ability.

Today there are more than three hundred breeds, each with its own special characteristics. The smallest breed, the *Falabella,* was developed by crossing a group of small English Thoroughbreds with Shetland ponies. Adult Falabellas weigh between forty and ninety pounds and are less than three feet high. These miniature horses are kept as pets and are sometimes trained for circuses.

The largest horses are the draft horse breeds. These huge work animals are descendants of the steeds that were originally bred to carry knights in armor. Most of these giants weigh more than a ton.

Midget Falabellas and giant draft horses are not appropriate riding horses. But Morgans, Arabians, or other breeds may be perfect for you. The most popular riding horse breeds in America are the Arabian, Quarter Horse, Thoroughbred, Morgan, American Saddlebred, Appaloosa, and Pinto. The most popular pony breeds are Shetland, Welsh, and Connemara.

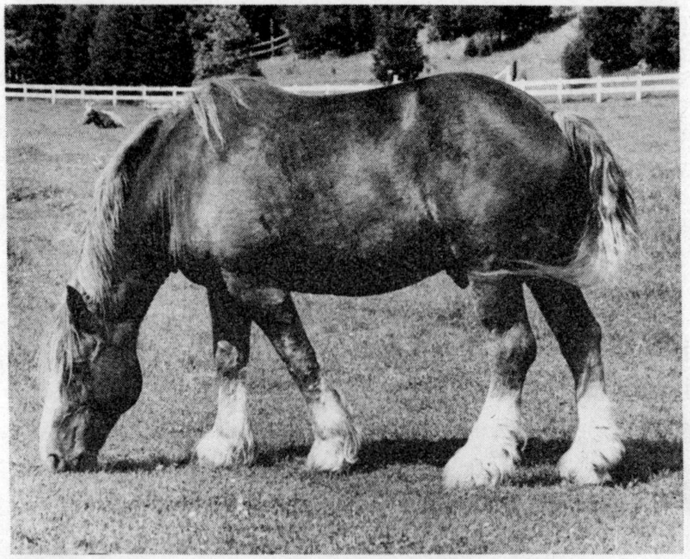

Draft horses are not for riding. They are used for farm work and for pulling heavy loads.

Each of these breeds has its own special qualities.

Horses of mixed breeding are called *grade* horses. They can make wonderful riding horses, and they are less expensive to buy than purebreds. Many grade horses are not as high-strung and sensitive as some of the purebreds.

Some people talk about "thoroughbreds" when they mean *purebreds*—that is, they may refer to an animal as a "thoroughbred Morgan," a "thoroughbred Shetland," and so on. This is the wrong term. A Thoroughbred, with a capital T, is a particular breed

These two horses, an Arabian (left) and a Thoroughbred, are examples of two popular riding breeds.

of horse that was developed in England during the eighteenth century. Purebred horses aren't necessarily Thoroughbreds. They can be any breed as long as the mother and father are members of the same breed. For example, there are purebred Morgans, purebred Arabians, and even purebred Thoroughbreds.

Male or Female?

Unless you are a serious horse breeder, don't buy a *stallion*. Stallions, which are breedable male horses, can be difficult to handle. *Mares* (females) and *geldings* (males that can't be bred) make more suitable riding horses.

Most male horses are gelded so they will be gentler

to ride and handle. Gelding is a simple operation that makes male horses unbreedable and usually calmer.

Temperament: Any Mean Streaks?

Your new horse should be calm, even-tempered, and well-mannered. Bad-tempered horses that kick and bite can be dangerous. Spend some time around your prospective mount to see if he has good manners and a personality you like. If he pins his ears back often, or lifts a hind leg and threatens to kick, the horse may be unreliable.

Training: How Well Trained Do You Want Your Horse to Be?

When you become an experienced rider, you may want the challenge of training your own horse. Training horses takes a great deal of patience and know-how. A *green* (inexperienced) person on a green (untrained) horse may mean black-and-blue injuries for the rider. Until you have years of experience, start out with a horse that is already trained.

Cost: How Expensive?

Prices vary. A gentle, backyard horse can sometimes be found for less than a thousand dollars, whereas a purebred can cost ten times that or more. The horse's age, breed, and degree of training affect the price.

Color?

Do you have your heart set on a black beauty? Are you looking for a golden Palomino? There are bays, grays, chestnuts, and a variety of spotted horses. Pintos have patches, Appaloosas have spots, and many gray horses have dapples (blended spots).

This spotted horse is an Appaloosa.

Some horses are marked with *blazes* (white stripes on their faces), *stars* (white patches on their foreheads), and *socks* (white leg markings).

There's an old cowboy saying: "A good horse is any color." It's true, a horse of any color will do—as long as it's gentle and healthy. With good quality food, regular exercise, and daily grooming, you can make a horse of any hue look beautiful.

Your Color Chart

Bay: Bays can be any shade of brown with black manes and tails.

Black: Black horses must have a solid black coat. They can have white markings on their heads and legs, but all other hairs are black.

Brown: Brown horses have a dark brown coat with a black mane, tail, and legs. Some shades of brown are also called *dark bay*.

Buckskin: Buckskins are yellowish-tan to light-brown with a dark brown mane and tail. Most buckskins have a black stripe running down their spines.

Chestnut: Chestnuts are reddish-brown with a brown mane and tail. The color may range from light golden-red to dark chocolate.

Dun: Duns are a darker shade of buckskin. Primitive horses are believed to have been dun-colored.

Gray: Gray horses are born a solid color (bay, brown, or chestnut). They turn gray as they grow new hair every spring and fall. Each new hair coat has more white hairs, until eventually the horse looks white.

Palomino: Palominos have gold-colored coats with white or light blond manes and tails.

Roan: Roans may have any color hair with white hairs mixed in. A *strawberry roan* has chestnut and white hairs; a *blue roan* has dark gray and white hairs; and a *red roan* has bay and white hairs.

White: True white horses are born white. Most horses that look white are actually gray horses that lightened with age.

Vetting Out

When you finally find a horse you'd like to buy, *have a veterinarian examine the animal.* You don't want to spend money on one that is lame or unhealthy. Even the sleekest, healthiest-looking horse can have serious problems that only a vet can detect.

Veterinarians can spot health problems you may not see.

Markings on Casablanca's teeth reveal that she is about ten years old.

When veterinarians "vet out" a horse, they check the animal's eyes, heart, lungs, legs, way of moving, and overall health. They look at the horse's teeth to determine his age. The size, shape, grooves, and markings of the teeth make it possible to tell a horse's age fairly accurately, because the teeth change predictably throughout a horse's life.

Usually when people buy an expensive horse, the vet takes X rays of the front legs to make sure there are no hidden problems. Because horses' front legs carry about 75 percent of their body weight, this is where most lameness problems occur. Vets bring a small portable X-ray machine, so that the horse can be X-rayed in his own barn.

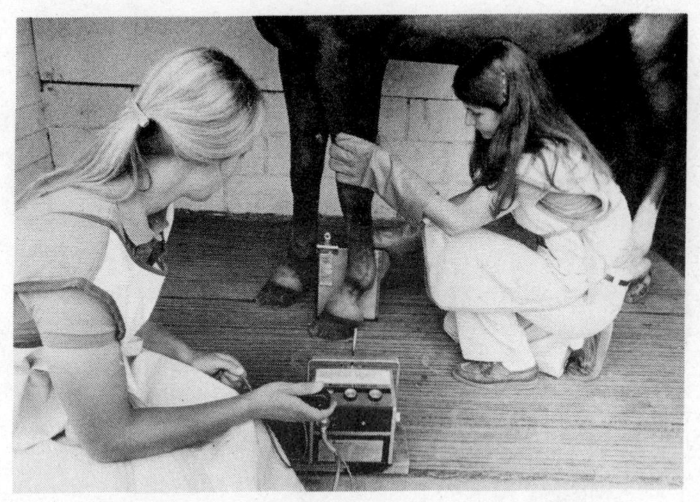

Dr. Koch and her assistant are x-raying a horse to check for hidden problems.

Where to Buy a Horse

To find a good horse to buy, you will have to make lots of phone calls and visit many farms. It can take a lot of time to find the perfect horse for you. Look for advertisements in local newspapers and horse magazines. Ads can also be found on bulletin boards at feed and tack stores.

Talk to veterinarians, farriers (horse shoers), riding instructors, stable managers, and neighbors. Many fine mounts have been found through the word-of-mouth recommendations of people who have or work with horses.

Private Horse Owners

Private horse owners are among the best sources. Many young people sell their horses because they outgrow them or they are going away to college. Sometimes people move and can't take their horses with them.

Be wary of a person who is selling a horse without a good reason—or you may be buying someone else's problem.

Horse Dealers and Riding Stables

Horse dealers and riding stables usually have wide selections, and if they don't have an animal suited for you, they can generally find one.

Dealers are anxious to find a horse you like—and they can be too eager to make a sale. Don't be pushed into buying a horse unless you are absolutely sure he's the one you want.

Breeding Farms

If you want a horse of a specific breed, breeding farms may be just the place to look. They usually have good selections of well-cared-for horses. Careful breeding and fine care are reflected in their prices. Breeding farms usually sell expensive horses. If the farm has a good reputation, though, it may be worth the price to purchase a mount there.

Auctions

Although bargain horses can be found, auctions are not for the inexperienced buyer. Auctions give little—if any—opportunity to ride the sale animals. Many people use auctions to get rid of horses that are lame or have bad habits.

Breed Sales

Sales sponsored by breeding farms can be a good source for quality, purebred horses, but you have very little contact with the animals. Unless you "know your oats," you might come home with a very expensive, and totally unsuitable, horse.

Gift Horses

Occasionally some lucky (or unlucky!) person is given a horse. A free horse sounds wonderful, and indeed it may be, but if the animal isn't healthy and sound, it can lead to heartaches and high vet bills.

Remember, it costs just as much to care for a gift horse as it does for one you buy.

CHAPTER TWO

Good Horsekeeping: Housing for Horses

Good housing is important for your horse's health and happiness. Your horse's home doesn't have to be fancy, but it must be comfortable, secure, and clean.

You can keep your horse at home if you have at

least two acres. Your horse will need a barn or shed and a fenced-in field for exercise, play, and grazing. Horses need room to roam, run, and kick up their heels.

Outdoor Shelters

Most horses are happiest and healthiest living in a large stall or three-sided shed that opens into a large pasture. Then they can come and go as they please. When flies bother them, they come indoors. When they feel like romping, they go out. The shelter protects them from sun, wind, rain, and flies.

An outdoor *run-in-shed,* or open stall, should allow 12 feet by 12 feet of space per horse. A salt block and a clean, fresh supply of water must be available at all times.

Horses are big drinkers, gulping from five to thirty gallons of water a day. Most horses weigh between 1,000 and 1,200 pounds. About three-quarters of this weight is fluid. Horses can become sick if they don't drink enough. Therefore, be sure your thirsty friend's buckets stay full.

Barns

If you plan to enter horse shows, you may want to house your horse in a barn, where it will be easier to keep him clean and shiny. Of course, he will still need to go out in a pasture for several hours each day. Horses that spend too much time in their stalls become restless and develop bad habits. Bored horses may chew wood, pace around their stalls, and become high-strung.

Ideally, stabled horses should be kept in *box stalls,* not *straight stalls.* Straight stalls are narrow. Horses have little room to move and are tied in them. Box stalls are larger (usually 12 feet by 12 feet), and horses are loose, not tied.

Although horses doze and rest standing up, they must lie down to go into a true deep sleep. Box stalls give horses plenty of room to lie down and stretch out their legs. If a stall is too small, the horse can become stuck, or *cast,* while lying down. Horses are cast when they get down too close to a wall and can't get up by themselves. It isn't easy helping 1,200 pounds of horse to stand up!

Stalls should be clean, airy, and deeply bedded with wood shavings or straw. Bedding absorbs moisture and cushions your horse when he lies down. Cement floors must be covered with thick layers of bedding because they are very hard on horses' legs.

Furnish the stall with a feed bucket, one or two water buckets (depending on how big a drinker he is), and a salt block. Salt blocks can be kept in holders that attach to stall walls.

The stall's window should be covered with strong screening to stop curious noses from poking through the glass. Light bulbs should be covered and out of the horse's reach.

Stable tools should be hung away from horses.

A good, secure door latch is important. Some horses are masters of escape and able to open many kinds of latches with ease. Make sure your latch is horseproof, or your mount is likely to find his way out into the wild, blue yonder.

Stalls must be cleaned every day. Remove all the wet bedding, and add fresh bedding as needed. Some horses are very neat, using only one area of their stall as a bathroom; others scatter their droppings everywhere.

Your manure pile should be easy to reach by wheelbarrow or truck, but far enough from the barn so that it won't attract flies. You may be able to find a garden center, farmer, or landscaper who will remove

A well organized tack room.

your pile periodically. Horse manure makes excellent fertilizer.

In addition to stalls, your barn should have special areas for grain, hay, bedding, stable tools, and riding equipment.

If your horse gets loose, he will almost certainly head for the grain. If he finds it, he will "eat like a horse" and could become very sick. *Always keep grain out of a horse's reach in ratproof cans or bins.* Metal garbage cans work fine.

Riding gear must also be kept out of your horse's reach—or your big pet may mark your tack with tooth and hoof prints.

Pasture

Allow at least one acre of pasture per horse. Fencing must be safe and secure, and the field must have some shade and be free of litter, tools, and equipment. Experienced horsekeepers know that if there is a way a horse can get into trouble, he will usually find it. If your fence has even one weak spot, he'll discover it. After all, grass is greener on the other side, isn't it?

Examine the pasture often to check for litter, loose wire, and other objects that could injure your steed. Also look for animal holes. Horses have been known to break legs in holes made by woodchucks and other burrowing animals.

Post-and-rail or wood plank fencing is the safest. Some types of wire are acceptable. *Never use barbed wire.* If a horse becomes tangled in it, he can be severely hurt. Strong wire mesh, with holes too small for hooves to get caught in, is safe for most horses. But be sure the wire is easy for your horse to see and that no sharp pieces stick out.

Never tether a horse. If he gets tangled in a rope or chain, it may mean disaster. A tangled horse is likely to panic and seriously injure himself. A pasture with secure fencing is the only safe place to turn a horse out.

By nature, horses are herd animals, and they like to live in groups. When several share the same field, they establish a "pecking order." Through occasional kicks and bites, the number one horse lets the other animals know he's the King—first in line for food and water. After the order is established, the horses learn to respect each other, and there is only an occasional fight. Just be sure that the lowest horse in the pecking order gets enough to eat and drink.

If there isn't another horse to keep yours company, your animal might like a pet goat or chicken as a companion. It sounds silly, but some high-strung racehorses share their stalls with chickens or goats. These barnyard pals keep them calm and content.

Boarding Stables

If you've never taken care of a horse, or if you don't have enough land, your horse should live at a boarding stable. Boarding stables can be good places to learn about horse care and riding, and they give you a chance to meet other horse lovers.

Ask veterinarians, farriers, tack and feed store owners, or horsey neighbors to recommend stables. In-

Most boarding stables take care of your horse for you.

spect stables carefully before making your decision. Are the stalls clean? Do the horses look well-cared-for and healthy? Is there a good, safe pasture?

Talk to the people who board horses there. Are they happy with the care their animals get? Is there a good riding instructor?

Wherever you decide to keep your horse—at home or at a boarding stable—you'll find that there is a special joy in caring for your animal. Seeing your healthy horse contentedly grazing in his pasture will bring you happiness. And even cleaning his stall will make you feel proud.

CHAPTER THREE

Feeding Time

Horses love to eat, and feeding time is their favorite time of day. Wild horses spend an average of twelve hours a day grazing. Between meals, they nap, stroll, run, and "horse around."

Although horses are large creatures, they have small stomachs. Therefore, they should be fed several meals a day, rather than one large one. Two or three meals a day are best.

Horses like routine. They should be fed at the same hours every day. They seem to have invisible alarm clocks in their bellies that go off just before feeding time. If dinner is late, they can become upset and unruly. Therefore, feed your animal on time: early in the morning and late in the afternoon. If your horse works hard, a noon meal can also be served.

How much food does your horse need? There is no simple rule. Each animal needs a different amount, depending upon his size and how much work he does. Some horses are "easy keepers" and don't need much to stay plump. Others can eat constantly and never get fat. Your veterinarian or an experienced horseperson can help you decide how much your horse should eat.

Kinds of Food

We all know that hay is for horses. Good quality hay is the most important part of your horse's diet. It should be clean, slightly green in color, leafy, and free from mold or dust. Because moldy hay can make your horse sick, check each bale. Good clean hay should smell sweet, not dusty and stale.

Grain is important food, especially for horses that work hard. Most horses need several pounds, two or three times a day. Grain supplies nutrients and vitamins that are important for young and hard-working horses. Horses that aren't ridden often don't need much grain if they are fed good quality hay.

Feed stores sell mixtures that combine several grains, such as oats, barley, and corn, with vitamins and minerals. These mixtures are suitable for most horses. Have your vet recommend the mixture that is best for your animal.

All horses need salt, especially in hot weather when they sweat. Provide a salt block for your horse to lick when he pleases. Salt blocks come in red, white, or blue—not for patriotic reasons. Red and blue ones have minerals mixed in with them; white ones are plain salt. Your vet can tell you which color block is best for your horse.

Horses that are fed good quality hay and grain usually don't need vitamin supplements. But animals that are undernourished, growing, or pregnant do.

Feeding Rules

Horses have very sensitive digestive systems. Anything they eat must travel through about 100 feet of intestines. They are prone to a digestive illness called *colic.* There are many different kinds of colic. Some are simple stomachaches, while others are so serious that they can cause death. Colic kills more horses than any other illness. To prevent colic and to keep your horse healthy, several feeding rules must be followed:

1. Never feed moldy hay or grain.
2. Store grain safely away from horses.
3. Always measure the amount of grain you give your horse.
4. Never change your horse's diet suddenly. If you switch from one kind of grain to another, do it gradually.

5. If you increase your horse's grain ration, do it gradually.
6. Wait one hour after feeding grain before exercising your horse.
7. Horses must be cool when they eat grain and drink water. They should not be sweaty and hot.
8. If your horse must be confined to his stall because of bad weather, lameness, or illness, cut his grain ration in half.

Scrub your horse's water buckets daily to keep them clean.

9. Except when your horse is hot and sweaty, fresh, clean drinking water must always be available.

If your horse won't eat his food, lies down and gets up repeatedly, bites at his belly, or acts restless and uncomfortable, he may have colic. Call your vet immediately.

CHAPTER FOUR

Good Grooming

Grooming not only makes your horse clean and shiny, but it also improves his health. Rubbing and brushing is good for his blood circulation and muscle tone.

While giving your horse a once-or-twice-over, you

Casablanca enjoys her daily grooming.

have a perfect opportunity to check him for lumps and bumps, scrapes and scratches. Minor cuts can be treated with first aid ointment. Unusual swellings or serious cuts should be reported to your vet.

Horses housed in stables should be groomed every day. Pasture-living horses don't need thorough daily groomings, because dirt and grease from their coats form an insulating layer that helps keep them warm and dry. However, don't neglect those who live outdoors. They still need regular attention. *Every horse should be groomed before and after each ride.*

When you groom, you have a chance to learn about your horse's personality. The animal learns to know you and appreciates your kind attention. Most horses enjoy their daily heavenly horse massages.

Grooming makes horses clean and shiny.

This grooming kit contains a dandy brush, body brush, curry comb, hoof pick, mane comb, rub rag, first aid ointment, sponge, sweat scraper, and fly spray.

Tools of the Trade

To groom a horse properly certain tools are needed:

Curry comb: An oval-shaped grooming tool used in a circular motion to loosen dead hair and dirt. Rubber or plastic curry combs are best; metal combs are too harsh.

Dandy brush: a stiff-bristled brush used to remove mud, dirt, and dried sweat. It is used with firm strokes in the same direction as the hair grows.

Body brush: a soft-bristled brush used all over the horse's body to remove dust and to bring out your horse's shine. This is the only brush that should be used on the face.

Rub rag: a towel or cloth used to rub the horse's hair and to smooth out the coat. Rub rags are great for removing sweat and for making hair shine.

Sweat scraper: a smooth metal blade used for removing excess sweat and water after bathing a horse.

Mane and tail comb: a comb for tending the mane and tail. Before combing your horse's locks, pick out snarls and tangles with your fingers. This prevents hairs from being pulled out and broken when you comb.

Hoof pick: a tool used for removing mud and dirt from the underside of hooves. Mud dries out hooves,

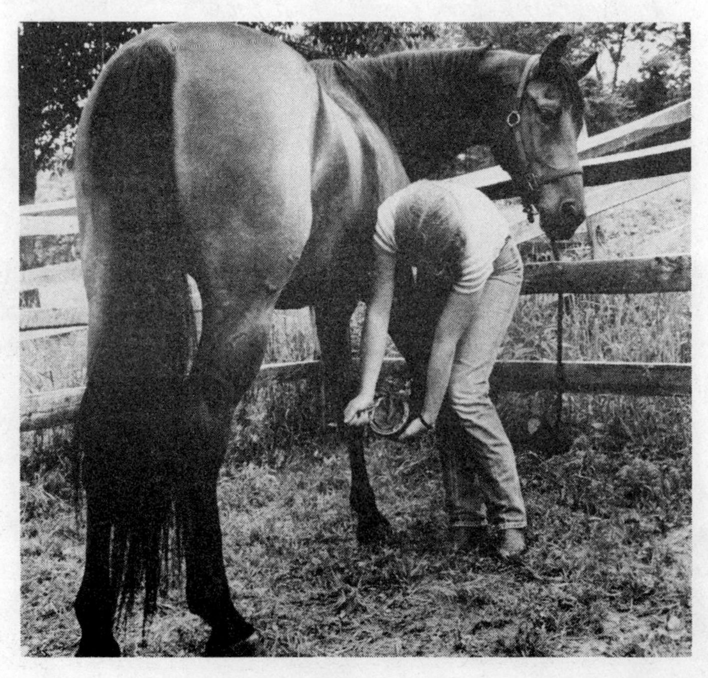

and a lodged stone can cause lameness. *Thrush,* a dark, smelly fungus, can develop in dirty hooves. Horses' hooves should be cleaned every day, and before and after every ride.

Hoof dressing: an ointment or oil used to keep moisture in hooves. Hoof dressing should be used a few times a week, depending on how dry your horse's hooves are. Your farrier can tell you how often to apply it.

Fly repellent: a spray, stick, or wipe used in the summertime to keep bothersome insects from bugging your horse.

First aid ointment: medication used to treat minor cuts and scrapes.

Box: for keeping all the above items handy.

Bath Time

Horse hair produces a natural oil, which makes the coat shine. By brushing, you distribute the oil over

your horse's body. When you shampoo, you remove the oil. Therefore, most of your grooming should be brushing, with only an occasional summertime bath.

If the weather is hot and your horse is dirty, it may be time to shampoo him. First dampen his body with a sponge or hose. (Be careful. Many horses seem to believe that hoses bite!) Then fill a bucket with warm water and mild shampoo. Rub your horse with a soapy sponge and rinse with plenty of clean water. Use a sweat scraper to remove as much excess water as possible.

Don't put your horse back in the stable until he is completely dry. Keep an eye on your squeaky clean

Sweat scrapers remove sweat and water.

horse. Wet horses love to roll—always in the dustiest or muddiest spots!

You'll never be too thrilled when your nice clean horse rolls in the slushiest patch of mud. But don't be

Some stables have special vacuum cleaners for horses.

too upset. The mud actually helps clean the horse's coat. As it dries and hardens, mud absorbs sweat and draws out impurities from the skin. When you finally manage to get all the mud off your horse (and probably onto yourself), you'll have a cleaner animal.

CHAPTER FIVE

Horseshoes

Horses need shoes for the same reason people need them—to protect their feet. The ancient Romans

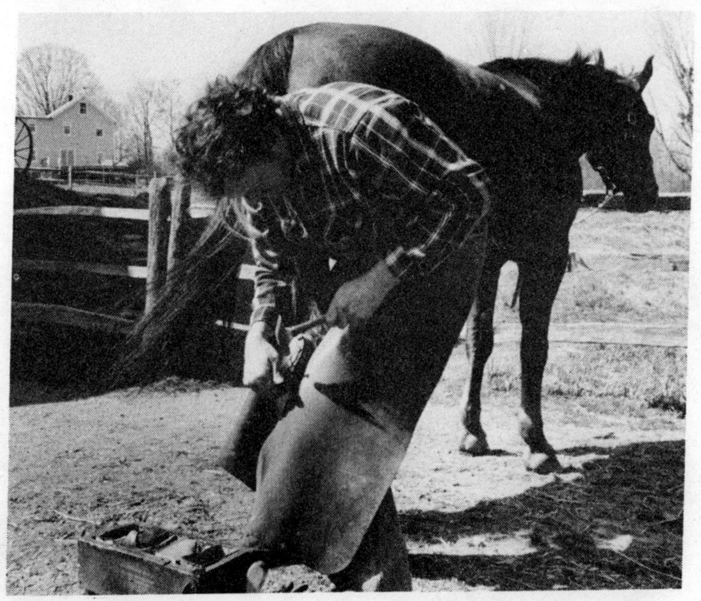

Eben, the farrier, shoes Damascus every six weeks.

used leather horseshoes; the Chinese made straw sandals for their mounts; and American Indians used leather moccasins, which they tied around their horses' ankles.

In days of old, people took their horses to the smithy to be shod. Today *farriers* (which is the correct name for blacksmiths who shoe horses) drive their well-equipped trucks right up to their customers' barns. They set up forges to heat metal and anvils to shape it. (*Anvils* are heavy iron blocks.) Metal horseshoes come in standard forms and must be custom-fitted to each horse. The shoe is first heated in the forge, then hammered on the anvil to the proper shape. When the shoe is cool, it is nailed onto the horse's hoof.

Eben shaping horseshoes on an anvil.

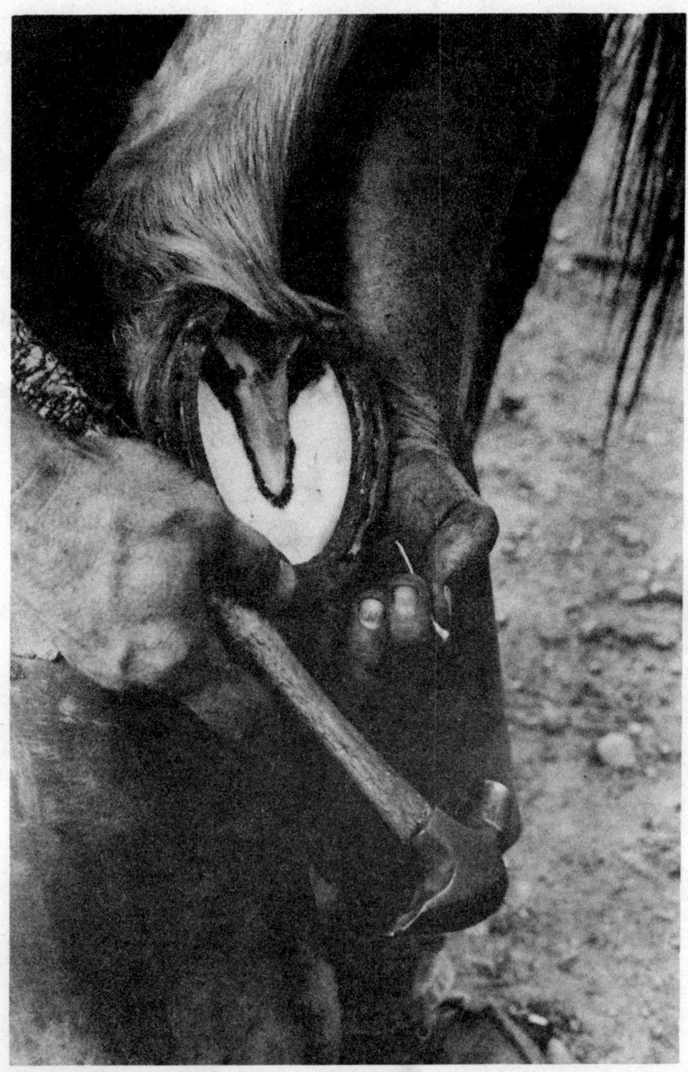

Horseshoes are held in place with special nails.

For winter use, shoes are made with metal cleats to prevent slipping on snow and ice. Some shoes have special studs that are screwed into the shoes for different riding conditions. If the ground is slippery and muddy, long, pointed studs are worn. If the ground is hard and grassy, small studs are needed.

Horses need to be shod every six weeks. Some ponies and horses that aren't ridden on hard surfaces don't need shoes, but they still must have their hooves trimmed every six weeks. Hooves, like fingernails, never stop growing. They need regular trimming to keep them from becoming too long.

CHAPTER SIX

Visits from the Vet

Even healthy horses need vets. Yearly shots, regular wormings, and periodic checkups help prevent illness. Vets are experts in animal care, and they should be consulted when you have important questions about your horse's health.

Routine Health Care

Your horse needs yearly shots that protect him against serious diseases. The shots your horse will need vary, depending upon where you live. Your vet knows which to give.

Once a year your vet will take a blood sample for a *Coggins test*. This reveals if your horse has *swamp fever*, a rare but dangerous disease. Swamp fever is also known as *equine infectious anemia*.

At least four times a year your horse will need *worming*. Worms, a common health problem, are one of the major causes of illness and death in horses. Horses must be wormed year-round. Even in the frozen north, horses need wintertime wormings. Many farms worm their animals every eight weeks.

Dr. Koch tests a horse's hoof for soreness.

Unfortunately, it's almost impossible to get rid of worms completely, but regular treatment can keep them under control. Surprisingly, even fat, shiny horses can be loaded with these crawling creatures.

Many types of worming medicines are available. Your vet may want a sample of manure to see exactly what kinds of worms your horse has so that he can prescribe the correct medication.

Periodically, a male horse needs his penis and *sheath* (the pocket of skin around it) cleaned. Your vet can advise you about this.

Tooth Care

Horses' teeth never stop growing, and sharp edges eventually form. These sharp, pointed teeth make chewing difficult, and can cause your horse to throw his head in pain when the bit is in his mouth.

Your vet should check your horse's teeth twice a

Teeth are floated (smoothed down) with long-handled files.

year. When edges are sharp, they can be filed down. To horsepeople, tooth filing is known as *tooth floating*.

Today there are special equine dentists who take care of horses' teeth. They file, float, and even pull teeth when necessary.

Signs of Illness

If your horse seems sick, injured, or lame, call your vet. It's best to catch problems early before they become serious. Here are some reasons to call your vet:

- If your horse loses his appetite, he probably isn't feeling well. Horses normally are extremely eager eaters.
- If your horse seems in pain, gets up and down repeatedly, rolls often (daily rolls are normal), kicks at his belly or bites at his sides, he may have colic.
- If your horse coughs frequently, has a runny nose, watery eyes, or difficulty breathing, he may have a cold or flu.
- If your horse has a temperature over 103 degrees (99–101 degrees is normal).
- If your horse has heat or swelling in a leg or foot, or if he is limping.
- If your horse has a severe wound that might need stitching.
- If your horse has diarrhea or doesn't pass manure for more than twelve hours.

Common Health Problems

Azoturia: Also called *Monday-morning sickness* and *tying-up,* azoturia affects horses that are worked hard, then left in their stalls on full grain rations the following day. The horse's muscles may become extremely stiff, he may not want to move, and his urine is brown. If you think your horse is suffering from azoturia, leave him in his stall and call the vet at once.

This illness can usually be prevented by cutting a horse's grain ration in half on days he won't be worked, and by making sure that he gets daily exercise.

Colic: There are many forms of colic, ranging from a simple stomachache to a twisted intestine. Because colic can be fatal, your vet should be called at the first sign of stomach trouble.

While waiting for the vet to arrive, quietly lead your horse around at a walk, and have a knowledgeable horseperson give your horse colic medicine recommended by your vet.

Most cases of colic can be prevented by careful feeding and regular worming.

Colds and flu: Horses get colds and flu just as people do. Even the symptoms are similar. Your horse may run a fever, cough, have a runny nose and watery eyes.

Flu shots are sometimes given to horses that go to shows often. These shots prevent them from catching the illness from other horses.

Cuts and scrapes: Horses often come in from the pasture with cuts and scrapes. Cuts should be cleaned with warm water and antiseptic soap, then treated with an antibacterial ointment or spray. *Furacin,* a yellow, germ-killing ointment, is commonly used to treat minor wounds.

If the wound looks serious, it may need stitching. Don't medicate it until the vet sees it.

Heaves: Horses that wheeze, cough, and have difficulty breathing may have heaves. Dusty hay, allergies, and poorly ventilated stables can cause heaves. Heaves can usually be prevented, but can't always be cured.

Lameness: Because horses are heavy animals standing on long, thin legs, they are subject to many kinds of lameness. Hot, swollen legs should be hosed with cold water, and the vet should be called. Sometimes injured or sore legs need wrapping with bandages. However, wrapping must be applied correctly or it can do more harm than good.

Lameness problems that are caught and treated early can usually be cured.

Saddle sores: Painful sores can be caused by improperly fitted tack, dirty saddle pads, or dirty horses. Careful grooming and clean, well-fitting tack will prevent them. If your horse does develop a sore under the saddle, stop riding him until it heals completely.

Strangles: This is a sickness that can easily be passed from one horse to another. It is called *equine distem-*

Dr. Koch wraps a lame horse's legs.

per or *shipping fever* (because horses that travel long distances are prone to it). Animals with strangles are sluggish, have a high fever, a thick nasal discharge, and swelling under the jaw.

A horse with strangles should be isolated from other horses and treated by a vet.

Thrush: If there is a thick, foul-smelling area in the bottom of your horse's hooves, he probably has thrush, a fungal infection. When your farrier shoes your horse, he can check for thrush and tell you how to treat it.

If caught early, thrush can be easily cured. However, if allowed to develop, it can make your horse lame. Horses that stand in dirty stalls or muddy pastures are likely to get thrush, but sometimes even the best-cared-for horses develop it. To prevent thrush, clean your horse's hooves every day and keep his stall clean.

Keeping Records

Every horse owner should keep a record of his horse's health history and shoeings. Write down the dates your steed is wormed, shod, vaccinated, has his teeth floated, and has any special treatments.

Use a calendar to mark down the dates your horse will be due for shots, worming, and shoeing. That way, you won't forget to keep his health care up-to-date.

Your First Aid Kit

Keep a supply of first aid items handy. Place a booklet or chart that describes first aid treatments near your medicine kit. And always have a knowledgeable horseperson help when you doctor your horse.

Your first aid kit should contain the following:

- antiseptic soap
- cotton and gauze for cleaning and dressing wounds
- antibiotic wound dressings: ointment, spray, and powder
- bandaging material for leg injuries
- adhesive tape
- scissors
- veterinary thermometer
- petroleum jelly
- liniment for sore muscles
- rubbing alcohol
- mineral oil
- antibiotic eye ointment
- any medications your vet feels you should keep on hand such as tranquilizer, colic medicine, and anti-inflammatory drugs (drugs that bring down swellings).

CHAPTER SEVEN

Tack: Equipment for Horses

Tack stores are filled with an astonishing assortment of bits, bridles, and saddles. Choosing the right tack (equipment) for your horse is an important and enjoyable chore.

Harnesses for horses were first used about 6,000 years ago in Asia. The first bridles were rawhide head straps with bits (mouthpieces) made of wood or horn. A simple cloth with a bellyband once served as a saddle.

Many kinds of saddles were invented over the centuries. Some saddles were nothing more than two cushions strapped together. Others were built like large chairs, with high rigid backs. Early American Indians didn't use saddles. Their only riding equipment was a thin strip of buffalo hide tied around the horse's jaw.

Today's modern saddles are made of leather with wood or fiberglass inside to make them hold their shapes.

Picking the right bit for your horse isn't always easy.

Saddles

A good saddle is important for riding comfort—yours and your horse's. The purpose of a saddle is to protect the horse's back and to help the rider stay balanced and comfortable. It is designed to rest on both sides of the horse's backbone. The saddle's inner framework, known as the *tree,* keeps it lifted off the horse's spine. A poorly fitting saddle can cause painful saddle sores on your horse's back.

There are two basic kinds of saddles—Western and English.

Western Saddles

Western saddles were originally designed for men working with cattle. Cowboys needed good, sturdy tack that could hold up to hard, everyday use. The

Western saddles (left) are much more elaborate than English saddles.

large *horn* on the front of the saddle was for attaching lariats. (A *lariat* is a long rope with a noose at one end for catching horses or cattle.) The high back, called the *cantle,* gave the cowboy back support for long rides and gave him a place to attach his bedroll and equipment. The wide flaps on the sides of the saddle protected the rider's legs from his horse's sweat.

Before the invention of the saddle horn, cowhands used trial and error to find a place for fastening the ends of their lariats. Some cowboys tried attaching them to their horses' tails! Others fastened them to poles, which they held. Many cowboys were pulled out of the saddle and onto the ground this way. Cowhands also attached lariats to the backs of their saddles or to large rings on the *cinches* (horse belly-bands). None of these methods worked too well.

Finally, the ingenious saddle horn was invented—certainly a much better place to attach a lariat than a tail.

For Western riders there are three main types of saddles:

Roping saddles: heavy-duty saddles designed for hard work and stress. Some may weigh close to fifty pounds.

Equitation saddles: designed for horse shows. These may be elaborately decorated with hand-tooled patterns, and may be inlaid with carved silver and gold.

General purpose saddles: ideal for pleasure and trail riding.

English Saddles

English style tack was originally designed for sports like foxhunting and horse racing. To enable horses to run fast and jump high, English saddles were made lighter, smaller, and less elaborate than Western tack. Although they were developed in Britain, these saddles have been used in the United States, Russia, France, Germany, and many other countries for more than a century.

These are the most popular saddles for English riding:

Forward seat saddles: designed primarily for jumping.

Dressage saddles: designed with straighter leg flaps to put the rider's legs close to his horse's sides so he can easily give cues.

All-purpose saddles: used for trail riding, jumping, and for elementary dressage. These are good saddles for beginners.

Saddle seat saddles: flat saddles that shift the rider's weight further back. These are used for riding horses with high-stepping leg action, like American Saddlebreds.

At one time, lady riders used *sidesaddles.* It was considered improper for a lady to wear pants and straddle a horse. There are still some women who enjoy riding sidesaddle for shows and foxhunts, but most modern women prefer to ride astride. Sidesaddle riders must carry a whip to replace the cueing function of the right leg.

Saddles come in different seat sizes. Tack stores

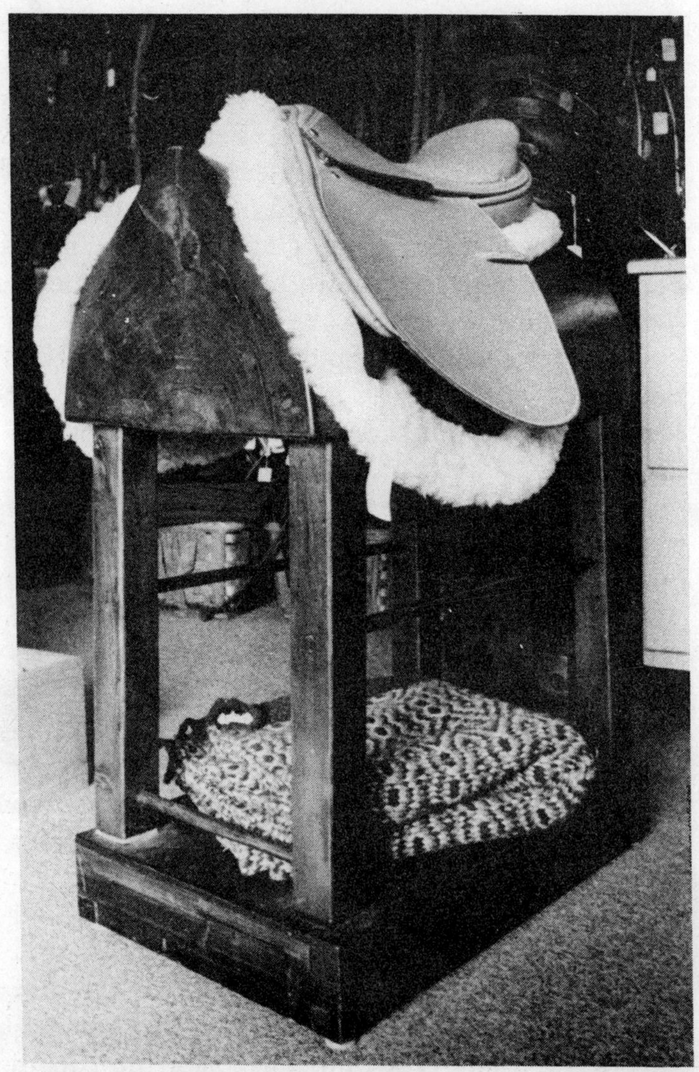

A wooden horse allows you to sit in a saddle before you buy it.

have wooden horses so that you can sit on several saddles to feel which fits best. The tack storekeeper can help you choose. If you are still growing, allow some extra room in the seat. You don't want to outgrow your saddle just when it's perfectly broken in and comfortable.

Saddles also come in different widths to fit horses' varied shapes. If possible, take the saddle home and try it on your (very clean) horse before you buy. The saddle should sit on the horse's back without touching his spine or withers. It's always wise to seek expert advice before buying.

Saddles are held in place with *girths* (English) or *cinches* (Western). These horse-sized belts may be made of leather, linen, cotton, cord, nylon, rayon, elastic, or mohair strands. Leather girths with elastic at one end are very popular with English riders. The elastic makes saddling easier, and it gives the horse's chest more room to expand when he breathes heavily.

Western cinches are usually made of cord. Many Western saddles have two cinches. The second cinch was devised to keep the saddle from slipping when cowboys rope cattle. It is never fastened as tightly as the front cinch.

Stirrups

Riders discovered a new security when the stirrup was invented. Stirrups are footrests that fasten to both sides of a saddle. They allow riders to turn in the saddle, shift their weight, and balance easily.

Your saddle's stirrups should be large enough so

your feet can easily slide out if you fall off. If you lose your balance, a caught foot can be extremely dangerous.

Saddle Pads

For your horse's comfort, use a saddle pad underneath your saddle. Saddle pads absorb sweat and cushion the animal's back. They also protect your saddle from dirt and sweat.

Pads are made from many different materials, and they come in an assortment of sizes and colors. They may be plain, plaid, pin-striped, or patterned. It doesn't really matter what style you prefer, but you must keep your pad clean and soft. Dirty pads can cause sore backs and skin problems.

Bits and Bridles

Thousands of years ago people discovered that by putting a bit in a horse's mouth, they could control the animal's speed and direction. Since this discovery, countless varieties of mouthpieces were invented. Some bits had spikes and were painful and cruel. Others were beautifully carved and inlaid with gold or silver. Regardless of design, all bits serve the same basic purpose. They are used to signal and control horses.

Horses have spaces several inches long between their front and back teeth. These spaces, called *bars,* are where the bit rests. The bars are very sensitive. Therefore, never pull suddenly or sharply on the reins.

English bit and bridle—plus a typical English riding hat.

Western bit and bridle—
plus a typical Western hat.

If your horse shakes his head or chomps on the bit, he may be in pain. Make sure the bit fits correctly and that you aren't pulling hard on the reins. If your horse is still uncomfortable, have your veterinarian check his teeth for dental problems.

A bit that fits properly shouldn't pinch. It should make just one wrinkle on each side of the horse's mouth.

Snaffle bits are the most commonly used bits. They consist of two rings connected by a straight, curved, or jointed mouthpiece. Some snaffles are gentle, but others, like the *twisted wire snaffle,* can be very severe and should be used only by skillful riders. The *egg-butt snaffle* is a favorite bit because it is comfortable for the horse.

Snaffles are a good choice for most riders, English or Western. However, it is important to remember that any bit can cause pain if it isn't used gently and properly. A rider's ability is much more important than the type of bit used.

A *curb bit* is stronger than a snaffle. Curb bits have side pieces, called *shanks.* When the reins are pulled, the bit turns in the horse's mouth. A short chain or strip of leather, worn under the horse's chin, is attached to the bit. This curb strap gives the rider more control by putting pressure on the horse's chin.

A *pelham bit* works like a snaffle and a curb bit combined. Because it is used with two reins, it can be hard to handle. One rein pulls the bit back (like a snaffle), the other rein turns it (like a curb). Some riders use a *bit converter,* a strip of leather that lets you use a pelham with one rein. But the trouble with this is that the bit can't be used correctly because it is designed for use with two reins.

Bridles are headpieces that hold the bit in a horse's mouth. Some riders use a bitless bridle called a *hackamore.* Hackamores apply pressure to the horse's nose instead of the mouth. Many trainers, both English and Western, use these for young horses and for horses with sore mouths.

With a properly adjusted bridle, you should be able to fit your fist under the throat latch and place one finger under the noseband.

Tack Care

Take good care of your tack. If it is kept clean and supple, tack can last for many years. Ideally, saddles, bridles, and girths should be cleaned after every ride. Use a damp, but not wet, sponge and saddle soap or glycerine soap. Then wipe your tack with a clean, dry towel. Rinse the bit in clean water and dry it.

If your saddle is mud-splattered after a ride, let the mud dry thoroughly. Then brush off the mud, and clean your saddle.

Leather needs oiling periodically to prevent it from drying out and cracking. Tack stores sell several kinds of oil that are suitable. Regular cleaning and occasional oilings will keep your leather soft, supple, and clean. Remember that dirty leather looks bad and can give your horse painful sores.

When you are not riding, keep your saddle on a saddle rack so that it will keep its shape. Hang your bridle on a curved bridle holder, not a nail. Nails cause leather to crack.

The Clothes Horse

Planning your horse's wardrobe isn't easy. A glance around a tack store will reveal a large assortment of horse clothes in many different colors and materials.

There are thick *wool coolers* for absorbing sweat and preventing chills, *rain sheets* for keeping your noble steed dry in wet weather, *fly sheets* for keeping biting insects off your animal, and an assortment of sheets and blankets to keep your horse warm in the colder months.

What does your horse need? To start, every horse needs a *halter* and a *lead rope.* Halters are used for leading and holding. They should be taken off when your horse is left in his stall or put out in his field. If left on, they can become tangled in brush or fencing, and they may cause sores and rubs on your horse's face.

If you live in a cold climate and plan to ride frequently in the winter, you will probably want to blanket your horse. Horses that spend winters in their "birthday suits" grow thick coats of hair. Blanketed horses usually don't. However, if your horse lives outside, it is best to let him grow his own furry coat.

Turn-out rugs are used on short-coated horses when they go outside in cold weather. *Sheets* are light horse blankets used in the spring and fall.

Wool coolers are good to have if you work your horse hard in cold weather. Sweaty horses can easily become chilled when it's cold. Coolers are put on after riding to keep the horse warm while his body cools off gradually.

If you plan to go to many horse shows, you may want to take along a rain sheet and a fly sheet. Otherwise, your horse can usually do without them.

CHAPTER EIGHT

Riding Right

Learning to ride correctly is important in order to enjoy your horse and to have your horse enjoy you. Riding is much more fun when you know what you're doing. It's also much safer!

You can usually find a good riding instructor at a 4-H Club, Pony Club, or riding stable. Everyone, no matter how talented, can benefit from lessons. Riding is a skill that can always be improved.

Debbie's riding instructor shows her how to hold the reins.

Two basic riding styles are used in America: English and Western. Westerners originally used their horses for working cattle and for transportation. They spent long, hard hours in the saddle, making their cow ponies stop, start, and turn quickly when rounding up cattle. Easterners used their horses mainly for transportation and sports like foxhunting, trail riding, and racing.

Both Easterners and Westerners developed their own special riding techniques. But horses are horses, and certain basic principles apply to all riders. Even if you are an experienced rider, it is good to review these basic principles.

A Western rider racing around barrels at a rodeo.

An English rider guides her horse over a jump.

Riding Basics

Riders signal their horses using four basic aids: their *hands*, *legs*, *seat*, and *voice*.

Hands are used to guide a horse's direction and to

help control speed. You should always maintain a gentle contact with the horse's mouth. Reins should never be jerked sharply. Horses' mouths are sensitive, and sharp pulls are painful.

A horse's power comes from his hind end. He balances himself with his forehand (front half). Your hands must follow the motion of his head and neck to help him balance himself and move freely.

A rider's legs control the horse's hindquarters. Legs signal horses to change gait, move faster, and turn sideways. Horses have a natural tendency to move away from pressure. That's why pressing your right leg against your horse's side should make him move left.

A rider's seat and weight help control the horse's speed and balance. By following the horse's motion with your seat, you help your horse stay comfortably in balance. Moving your seat forward usually signals a horse to go faster. (Did you ever notice the position of jockeys galloping racehorses? *Forward!*)

When giving vocal commands, your tone of voice is much more important than the actual word. A calm, soothing "Whoa" should make your horse slow down, while a clucking noise made with your tongue against the roof of your mouth should signal an increase in speed. Never scream or shout at your horse. You will only frighten him.

Most riding problems are caused by the rider, not the horse. Be sure your signals are correct and not confusing. Most mounts are willing to please, but they must understand your commands. With lessons, practice, and patience, you will learn to ride in harmony with your horse.

Riding Position: Head to Toe

Correct position varies for different types of riding and for different speeds, but the following basic position applies to all riders.

Head should be up, with eyes looking forward. The back should be straight but not stiff. Shoulders should be back, arms relaxed. (To place your shoulders and arms correctly, lift your shoulders up, pull them back, and let them drop down. Then bend your elbows to form a straight line from the bit and reins to your elbows.)

Thighs should rest against the sides of the saddle. Knees and ankles, which act as a rider's shock absorbers, should be flexed. The ball of the foot should rest on the stirrup, and the heel should be lower than the toe. The toe points straight ahead, not in or out. If the leg is placed correctly, the stirrup leather will hang straight down.

English riders hold the reins in two hands; Western riders hold them in one. (Working Western riders need to keep one hand free for ranch chores like roping cattle and fixing fences.)

The correct Western leg position.

The correct English leg position.

CHAPTER NINE

Trail Riding

Trail riding is one of the greatest riding pleasures. Being on a runaway horse in the middle of the woods is not! Before hitting the trail, you should be able to control your horse in a confined area. For your safety and enjoyment certain rules should be followed.

Rules of the Road

1. Ride along the road only if your horse is not bothered by loud noises and traffic. Horses that frighten easily can be very dangerous near autos and trucks. In general, avoid busy roads.
2. When riding on pavement, walk your horse. Horses should never be asked to go fast on pavement because it is slippery and hard on their feet.
3. Ride single file and allow one horse length between horses. If you don't do this, your horse may get bitten from behind or kicked by the horse in front.
4. Don't ride after dark. Because nighttime vision is poor, accidents can occur.

Rules of the Trail

1. Whenever you ride, whether on a trail or in a ring, walk the first mile (five to ten minutes) and the last mile. Horses need time to warm up before working, and time to cool down afterward. If your horse is still hot when you return, get off and walk him until he is no longer hot and sweaty.

2. Don't ride on lawns or planted fields. Be considerate of your neighbors.

3. Leave every gate the way you found it. If it was closed when you came, make sure it's closed when you leave.

4. Walk your horse if the ground is muddy, rocky, steep, or uneven. Remember that although horses are big, strong animals, they can become lame quite easily.

5. When riding uphill, lean slightly forward to help your horse stay in balance. When going downhill, sit up straight.

6. *Never ride double*. Horses' kidneys are beneath their loins right behind the saddle. The kidneys are unprotected and can be damaged by the weight of a second rider.

7. When riding on a trail, be aware that any unfamiliar looking object may make your horse shy. (*Shy,* in this case, means to bolt because of fear.) Because horses' eyes are set wide apart, they can see almost all the way around themselves. (In the wild, horses depend on this well-rounded vision to spot danger.) Horses may react instantly to a movement or

object that they think may hurt them—even though it's just a fluttering piece of paper or a silly old rock. If your horse shies, sit deep in the saddle and stay calm.

Cooling Out After the Ride

If your horse is sweaty or hot when you return from a ride, you must cool him out properly before returning him to his stall or pasture. *Cooling out* means

Casablanca wears a sweat sheet so she won't catch a chill as she cools off.

walking your horse until his body temperature returns to normal. When the horse's chest feels about the same temperature as the rest of his body, he is cool. Horses that aren't thoroughly cooled out can become sick or lame. Your favorite mount may turn into a sore "charley horse."

In hot weather you can sponge your horse with water to help him cool down. Use a sweat scraper to remove excess sweat and water. In cold weather, rub him with a dry towel to remove sweat. You might want to place a cooler over him to prevent chills.

Always allow plenty of time after riding to cool out your horse. *Hot horses should never eat grain or gorge themselves on water.* Small sips of water are okay, but long drinks shouldn't be permitted until his body temperature is normal.

CHAPTER TEN

Show Time

After you have been riding awhile you may want to enter a horse show. Horse shows enable you to mea-

A formal dressage salute.

sure your riding ability. They also give you a good opportunity to meet other horsey people.

Before the Show

Preparing for a show means hours of work. Your horse should be bathed, have his whiskers clipped,

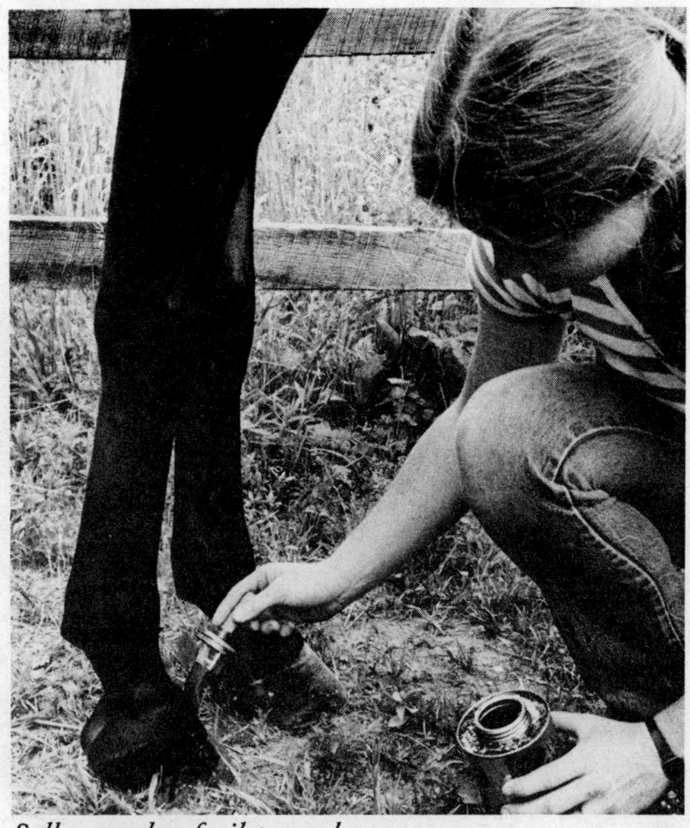

Sally uses hoof oil to make Squirt's hooves shine.

hooves oiled or polished, and, in some cases, his mane braided with yarn, thread, or rubber bands.

Horses wear their manes and tails in a variety of ways. The styles of hairdo depend upon the type of show entered and the horse's breed. For example, Arabian horses wear long, flowing manes and tails, but Thoroughbreds usually wear short, braided manes and often have braided tails.

The day before the show, you should clean your tack, polish your boots, and make sure all your equipment is clean and ready.

Before leaving for the showgrounds, the horse's legs are wrapped with padding and bandages to

This horse's mane is braided and wrapped with white tape.

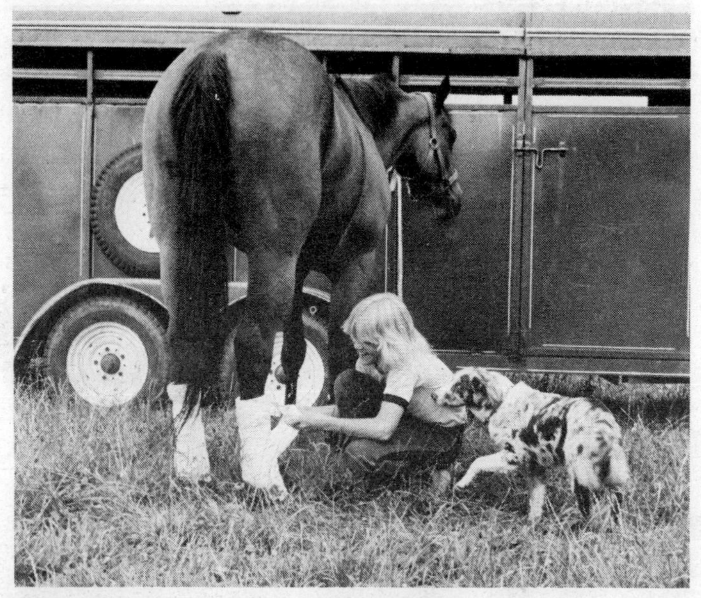

Tracy wraps her horse's legs before putting him in the horse trailer.

protect them during the trailer ride. Some horses wear special head bumpers that cushion their heads in case they rear up in the trailer.

Horse Show Classes

There are horse shows of many different levels, so that children on shaggy ponies can compete, as well as professionals on well-polished horses.

Here are some of the most common classes found at horse shows:

English Classes

Hunter classes: The horse's performance and manners are judged. There are *flat classes*: no jumps; just walk, trot, canter, and (sometimes) gallop. And there are *jumping classes*. Hunter jumps are similar to jumps found in the hunting field—gates, brush, post-and-rails, and coops.

Equitation classes: The rider's skill and form are judged in these classes. The horse is not judged. There are flat and jumping equitation classes with many divisions for riders from beginner to advanced.

Jumper classes: These test how high, wide, and sometimes how fast a horse can jump. Jumper courses

This horse clears a big jump at a horse show.

usually contain colorful combinations of high, closely placed jumps.

Pleasure and trail classes: The horse's manners and suitability as a pleasure or trail horse are examined.

Saddle Horse classes: The horse's performance at his high-stepping gaits are judged. In *combination classes,* Saddle Horses are driven in harness, then tacked-up and ridden English style.

Saddle Horses are known in the show ring for their flashy, animated leg action. They were originally used as mounts for Southern plantation owners who spent countless hours in the saddle and needed horses with smooth, ground-covering strides.

Western Classes

Stock seat equitation: Riders are judged during the walk, jog (trot), and lope (canter). In some classes, contestants may be tested in other ways, such as riding without stirrups or performing figure-eight patterns.

Stock horse classes: Horses ride through patterns containing figure-eight, spins (fast turnarounds), roll-backs (backing up), and other maneuvers. In some stock horse classes, a calf is released inside the show ring so that horse and rider can demonstrate their ability to work cattle.

Trail horse classes: Riders guide their mounts through obstacles similar to those they would find on the trail. They may, for example, have to ride through water, cross a bridge, open and close a gate, and back up between obstacles.

Pleasure horse classes: The horse must walk, jog, lope, and back up while ridden on a fairly loose rein.

Gymkhana classes—games on horseback: There are, for example, *barrel races* (where horse and rider are timed as they gallop around a course of barrels), *pole bending* (where riders, one at a time, race through a succession of poles), and *relay races.* In some relay races, riders carry an egg in a spoon or a glass of water while they ride.

Some shows also offer *bareback classes* and *costume classes,* in which riders dress themselves and their horses in any costume that takes their fancy.

Dressage Shows

Dressage is the art of training a horse in obedience and in precise movements. The rider signals com-

Dressage horses are graceful athletes.

mands by subtle movements of hands and legs and by slightly shifting his weight. Dressage horses should perform gracefully and willingly. When correctly presented, dressage is a beautiful spectacle of horse and rider performing in complete harmony.

At dressage shows, riders execute riding patterns that they memorized long before the show. Movements range from simple circles at the trot and canter, to *half-passes* (the horse crosses his legs while moving forward and sideways) and *pirouettes* (the horse canters a tiny circle revolving around his own hind legs). The rider's commands should be practically invisible as the horse flows from one movement to another.

At the beginner level of dressage, riders perform simple patterns that don't require fancy steps.

Eventing

Beauty and grace, speed and courage, skill and suspense—all are found in Eventing. It's an exciting sport that tests many different skills.

Each horse and rider performs a *dressage test*. Then there's a gallop over a long *cross-country course* filled with obstacles, such as ditches, stone walls, and water jumps. *Stadium jumping* is the third and final test. Each horse takes a winding course over brightly painted jumps. Scores from these three tests are added together in order to find the winners.

Events are also called *horse trials* and *combined training*. The sport developed from tests that were given to European cavalry officers. Army horses had to be obedient and calm during ceremonies and

Jennifer and her horse leap off a bank jump during an event.

parades. This meant that they needed dressage skills. They had to be fit and bold to carry their riders over long distances, across mud, rocks, and hills, through forests and fields, over fences, streams, farm equipment, and any other obstacles in their way. They developed cross-country skills in this way. And the horses had to be willing to jump obstacles even when tired from a full day's work. The best rehearsal for this was stadium jumping.

Whether you decide to show, event, trail ride, or just ride now and then, you'll find that being involved with horses is a wonderful, rewarding experience.

Sir Arthur Conan Doyle's

THE ADVENTURES OF SHERLOCK HOLMES

Adapted for young readers by Catherine Edwards Sadler

Whose footsteps are those on the stairs of 221-B Baker Street, home of Mr. Sherlock Holmes, the world's greatest detective? And what incredible mysteries will challenge the wits of the genius sleuth this time?

A Study In Scarlet In the first Sherlock Holmes story ever written, Holmes and Watson embark on their first case together—an intriguing murder mystery.

The Red-headed League Holmes comes to the rescue in a most unusual heist!

The Man With The Twisted Lip Is this a case of murder, kidnapping, or something totally unexpected?

Join the uncanny and extraordinary Sherlock Holmes, and his friend and chronicler, Dr. Watson as they tackle dangerous crimes and untangle the most intricate mysteries.

AVON CAMELOT

AN AVON CAMELOT ORIGINAL • $2.50/$3.25

(ISBN: 0-380-78089-5)